CW00850856

Also available:
MY FAVOURITE NURSERY RHYMES
MY FIRST NURSERY STORIES

First published in Great Britain in 2010 by Andersen Press Ltd.,
20 Vauxhall Bridge Road, London SW1V 2SA.
Published in Australia by Random House Australia Pty.,
Level 3, 100 Pacific Highway, North Sydney, NSW 2060.
Copyright © Tony Ross, 2010
The rights of Tony Ross to be identified as the author and illustrator
of this work have been asserted by him in accordance with the
Copyright, Designs and Patents Act, 1988.
All rights reserved.
Colour separated in Switzerland by Photolitho AG, Zürich.
Printed and bound in Singapore by Tien Wah Press.

10 9 8 7 6 5 4 3 2 1

British Library Cataloguing in Publication Data available.

ISBN 978 1 84270 980 1

This book has been printed on acid-free paper

MY FAVOURITE FAIRY TALES

Retold and illustrated by

TONY ROSS

ANDERSEN PRESS

CONTENTS

THE HEDLEY KOW

EVERY day, Old Mary climbed out of her cold bed and ate her breakfast, which was always part of yesterday's supper. Then, she set out to walk down the lane because one day, she thought, she would find something good enough to sell, and then she could buy some new food.

"How lucky I am," she thought, "to perhaps one day find something that may be valuable! Lucky me!"

Anyway, this was a SPECIAL day, because Old Mary DID find something. She found an old pot.

"Hmmm," thought Old Mary. "That pot must have a hole in it, or nobody would leave it lying about like that. Lucky I didn't waste my time picking it up!" and on she hobbled.

Then she stopped, and went back. "Even with a hole in it, I may find a use for it," she thought, and examined the pot.

Imagine Old Mary's surprise when she found the pot stuffed with golden coins!

"Well, I'm blessed with luck to find this!" she chuckled, and she tried to pick up the pot. But gold is heavy, and Old Mary could not lift it, so she tied her shawl to the pot, and started to drag it home.

After a time, she looked back at the pot of gold, and found to her surprise, that it had turned into a lump of silver.

"That's lucky," she thought, "since silver is less valuable than gold, I am much less likely to be robbed. Oh, how lucky I am!" And she went on her way.

After a while, the silver seemed to get heavier and heavier, and Old Mary stopped to examine it, only to find that her lump of silver had turned into a bigger chunk of rusty iron.

"Bless my soul!" cried Old Mary. "I am the luckiest woman in this world. There is a blacksmith near here, who will give me pennies for that iron, and pennies are much less likely to be stolen than silver. How lucky I am!" And so she dragged her chunk of iron happily on towards her cottage.

When Old Mary got to her front door, she sat down on her chunk of iron to catch her breath, only to find it had turned into a rock. She clapped her hands with joy. "That rock is JUST what I have always wanted to prop my door open in the warm weather, and the good thing is, I don't have to drag it all the way to the blacksmith's. Oh, how lucky I am!"

She pushed the rock up to her door, and stood back to admire it, and to think about her good fortune.

Just then, the rock turned into the Hedley Kow, who trotted away down the lane, laughing at his silly trick. You see, the Hedley Kow was a fairy trickster, who had changed himself into the pot of gold in the first place, and decided to have some fun with whoever came along the lane.

Old Mary watched him skipping away down the lane.

"Folks around here have heard of the Hedley Kow," she said to herself, "but I'm the only one who has seen him. Oh, how lucky I am!"

Smiling, Old Mary went indoors to think of all her good luck.
"Oh, if only I could have such a lucky day tomorrow . . ."
she thought, as she dozed contentedly by her fire.

The Musicians of Bremen

ONCE there were four animals: a cockerel, a cat, a dog and a donkey. They had worked hard all their lives, and the time had come for them to have some fun.

"Let's teach dancing!" said the cockerel.

"No," said the cat, "we could be actors!"

"We all have beautiful voices," said the dog. "Why don't we sing opera?"

"N-o-o-o-o," brayed the donkey, "we all have g-r-e-a-t talents. Let us go to B-r-e-m-e-n. We could form a band!"

"Bags I the banjo!" mewed the cat.

"With me on bagpipes!" barked the dog.

"The flute's about my size", crowed the cockerel.

"And with me on drums, we can't f-a-i-l," brayed the donkey.

So off they set.

As none of the animals had any instruments, they made up wonderful songs on their way. They crowed and mewed and barked and brayed their songs to each other, until the sun began to sink in the forest. It grew darker and darker, and the animals fell silent, wondering where they were going to spend the night. In a clearing, they came to a hovel, with lighted windows.

The dog jumped onto the donkey's back, and the cat scrambled onto the dog's back. The cockerel flapped up on top of the other three, and peeped into the window.

"There are four men in there," crowed the cockerel.

"Perhaps it's a b-a-n-d," brayed the donkey, from down below.

"Perhaps they have instruments?" purred the cat.

"I don't think so," said the cockerel. "They seem to have guns and knives and sticks, bags of money, and lots of food. I think they are scallywags and fearful robbers!"

"P-e-r-h-a-p-s they are kindly robbers and, if we sang nicely, they would give us some food," whispered the donkey.

All of the animals agreed that was a good idea. And so, standing in the moonlight, on each other's backs, the four animals sang their new songs at the tops of their voices. They all sang different words to different tunes.

To the musicians' surprise, the hovel door flew open, and the four robbers stumbled into the moonlight.

"Well," muttered the Donkey, "w-h-a-t-'s all that about?"
The animals watched the robbers disappear down the darkened path.
"Never mind!" they thought, and they went into the empty hovel, ate the food, and settled down to rest.

Later that night, one of the robbers crept back to see if it was safe to return, and he saw the cat's eyes shining in the dark. Thinking them to be coals, dying in the fire, he reached out with his candle, and tried to light it with the cat's face. Then, in a blink, all madness happened.

The frightened cat swiped out with her claws, scratching the robber's nose. The dog bit the robber on the leg, the donkey kicked him on the bottom, and the cockerel chased him out of the door, screaming,

"Cock a doodle dooo . . . I'll get YOU!"

The terrified robber ran helter-skelter back to where his friends were hiding. "It's worse than we thought," he gasped. "The place is FULL of MONSTERS! There's a horrible witch who scratched my nose with her long, spiky fingers, a wicked dwarf with a knife who cut my leg, a fearful ogre who battered my bottom with his club and, worst of all, a demon swooped down from the roof, screaming at me!"

The other robbers listened to this account with some dismay, and agreed to run as fast as they could, away from the hovel, and never ever go near it again.

So, the animals lived there happily together for the rest of their lives. They never did get a flute, a banjo, bagpipes or drums, and even if they had, they wouldn't have been able to play them. Instead, they practised their singing, and became very good indeed. In time, their fame spread far, and they became known as The Musicians of Bremen.

SWEET PORRIDGE

BESS was a poor, poor girl, who was, by the way, a good and dutiful daughter. She and her mother lived together, in a poor little house, in a poor little street. Times were always hard, but the winters were the hardest.

In winter, Bess and her mother were not only cold, but hungry too. Sometimes they found little things to eat, things that their neighbours had thrown away, but as the frost hardened, there was less and less in the dustbins.

At last, they only had one small oat cake left, so Bess's mother said, "Bess, there are no two ways about it, you must go into the forest to find something to eat, or otherwise we will surely starve. Here, take half of this oat cake to keep you going."
So Bess wrapped herself in her warmest rags, and set off into the forest.

After an hour, she had found nothing, and was just thinking that she had better eat her half oat cake, when she stumbled across a tiny old woman, crouching in the snow. The old woman put out her hands and cried, "Don't pass me by, I am hungry. Please, please, do you have any small scrap to eat?"

Although hungry herself, Bess felt sorry for the old woman, and gave her half of her half oat cake. The old woman smiled, and then stood up. She seemed taller now, and not so old. "You are a kind child," she said to Bess. "I have asked a hundred travellers to share what they had with me, but they all said they had too little. You have less than any of them, but you would give half to me. I would like you to have this, as a reward for your kindness." And so saying, she handed Bess a small brown pot.

"Cook, little pot, COOK!" said the old woman, and the pot instantly filled up with porridge.

"Stop, little pot, stop!" said the old woman, and the pot stopped filling up. Bess and the old woman sat together in the snow, and ate the delicious hot porridge.

"Never part with that pot," said the old woman. "Then you will never be hungry again. Do you remember what to say?"
"I do!" said Bess. "Cook, little pot!" Nothing happened. "It doesn't work for me!" she wailed.
"Of course it does," smiled the old woman. "You got the words wrong. You must say, 'Cook, little pot, COOK!'"
Immediately the pot began to fill with porridge. "Stop, little pot, stop!" shouted Bess, clapping her hands, and the pot stopped.

Bess hugged her pot so tightly, she did not notice the old woman fade away.

Her mother was excited and happy with the pot, and delighted to see it work. From that day on, whenever they were hungry, Bess said, "Cook, little pot, cook!" And when they had eaten their fill, Bess said, "Stop, little pot, stop!" and the porridge stopped.

Stop, little pot, stop!

Sometimes the neighbours would pop in, drawn by the wonderful smell of hot porridge, and there was always some for them too. But Bess and her mother were careful only to use their enchanted pot when nobody was looking. They spent the happiest and warmest winter of their lives.

One day, Bess was out finding sticks for the fire, when her mother felt like a mid-morning snack. She took the pot from its hiding-place, and said, "Cook, little pot, cook!" Of course, the pot began to fill with porridge. "All right, ENOUGH!" shouted Bess's mother after a while. But the porridge kept coming.

"STOP!" shouted Bess's mother, but the pot overflowed, and began to fill the room with delicious porridge. She put the pot into a cupboard, shouting, "No more, NO MORE!" but the porridge bubbled out of the pot, and spilled out of the cupboard. In no time at all, the poor little house was full of porridge. "NO, NO, NO, NO!" screamed Bess's mother as the street began to fill with porridge.

As all the other houses filled with porridge too, the neighbours ran hither and thither, trying to escape the sweet tasty stuff.

Bess heard their screams, and came running back, but by this time the whole street was buried in porridge.

Bess waded through the porridge, and found the enchanted pot. "STOP, LITTLE POT, STOP!" she cried, and, at once, the obedient little pot stopped.

Slowly the neighbours returned, one by one, to their houses in the little street. They had to eat their way in. Of course, the porridge was cold by now, but it was still delicious.

In fact it was so delicious that they all grew quite fat,
and no one ever went hungry again.

RUMPELSTILTSKIN

ONE day, a king was touring his kingdom, when he arrived at the tumbledown cottage of a poor weaver.

"I may be poor now," said the weaver, "but one day I will be rich beyond dreams."

"Why is that?" asked the King, suddenly interested.

"Well, Your Majesty," lied the weaver, who wanted to impress the King, "I have a wonderful daughter, who has just been taught by the fairies how to spin straw into gold!"

"Then I'll take her with me," said the King. "If she can do as you say, then I will marry her, but if she can't, then it will be the worse for you."

The King locked the poor girl in a room in a deserted tower. There was nothing in the room but a bale of straw and a spinning-wheel. "There you are," said the King. "I'll come back in the morning for the gold."

Of course, the girl could not spin the straw into gold, so she sat there and wept, dreading the King's return.

Suddenly, a strange little goblin appeared, and asked the reason for her tears. When the girl explained, the goblin laughed. "Is that all? Why, I can do that in a twinkle, and all it will cost you is your fine necklace." Although her mother had given her the necklace, the girl handed it over. Soon she fell asleep to the hum of the spinning wheel. When she woke up, the goblin was gone, but, true to his word, there was a pile of gold where the straw had been.

The King was delighted. He took the gold, and brought more straw. "There you are. See what you can do with that," he said. So, the weaver's daughter waited until the evening, and the goblin returned.

"I'll spin that into gold for you," he said, "and all it will cost you is that pretty ring on your finger." The girl agreed, although the ring had also been a present from her dear mother. As the spinning wheel sang its song, she fell asleep.

When she woke up, there was more gold where the straw had been.

The King hopped with excitement, and he filled the room with straw. The girl stared at the straw, and waited for the goblin to return, which he did, as soon as it was dark. But the poor weaver's daughter had nothing more to give. "That's quite all right," whispered the goblin. "I'll spin all of this into gold, and all it will cost you is your first-born child." Of course, the girl quickly agreed – she had no husband, nor could she think of getting one. Once again, she fell asleep to the tune of the spinning wheel, and woke up to find the room filled with gold.

The King was so excited at his new wealth, he married the poor weaver's daughter that very day.

As the years rolled by, the King and his Queen had a beautiful baby daughter, and the kingdom rejoiced. They were as happy as any parents could be, until the awful night when the goblin returned. The King was away hunting, and the Queen had quite forgotten about the promise she had made to the goblin.

"I've come for the baby," he said. "You know, there was an agreement, and you are bound by that."

The Queen sobbed and pleaded with the goblin, but his mind was made up. "The agreement was your first-born," he insisted, pointing to the baby, "and agreements must be kept!"

The Queen clung to the goblin's knees. "Don't take my baby!" she sobbed. "I'll give you my half of the kingdom and all my riches!"

"Tell you what," said the goblin, "I've got a better idea. Did I ever mention my name?"

"No," said the Queen.

"Well, it is an unusual name, and if you can guess what it is, then you are released from our agreement."

"Is it Archibald?"
"No," said the goblin.
"Timothy, Pancho, Balmoral?"
"No, no, no!" sniggered the goblin. "I'll go now and come back tomorrow, and if you can guess my name, then you can keep your daughter."

When he was gone, the Queen knew that she could never guess the mysterious name, so she sent for her servant.
"Somewhere on the road, you will find an ugly little man. Follow him, and see if you can find out what his name is," she commanded. So the servant set off.

Later that night, the servant returned, grinning all over his face. "I followed him to a little shack, deep in the forest," he said, "and there I heard him singing this song:

Today I bake, tomorrow I brew,
The day after that, the Queen's child comes in,
And oh! I am glad that nobody knew,
That the name I am called is Rumpelstiltskin!"

"Rumpelstiltskin, Rumpelstiltskin!" the Queen sang happily,
dancing round the room, hugging her baby.

Early next day, the little goblin appeared before the Queen, in her tower.

"Good morning, Rumpelstiltskin!" she smiled.

The goblin stopped in his tracks, knowing he could never now take the baby. His face went red, and he spluttered terrible words.

Then to the Queen's amazement, he ran round the walls, spitting and squealing, only to vanish out of the window like a balloon when you take your fingers off the nozzle.

Nothing was ever heard of him again. As for the King and the Queen and the baby Princess, they lived happily together for ever.

PRINCE HYACINTH AND THE DEAR LITTLE PRINCESS

ONCE upon a time, the King of a faraway country fell in love with a beautiful princess. However, a spell prevented her from ever marrying.

The King wandered around his kingdom sadly, looking for an answer to this problem, until one day he came across a fairy, disguised as an old woman.

"ₐAAAAAHHH, YES!" cackled the old woman. "I know all about that Princess. She is held prisoner by a wicked magician. He has changed himself into her cat, so that he can always keep an eye on her. All you have to do is step on the cat's tail, and his hold over her will be broken. She CAN be yours. Good luck."

So the King went back to the Princess, and stepped on her cat's tail. With a horrible miaow, the cat turned into the magician, breaking the spell.

As the happy couple turned to leave, the magician screamed with rage, "You THINK you will be happy? NO! Your only child will have the saddest life, for ever and ever and ever . . ."

The magician's voice grew smaller, as he turned into a mouse, and ran down a hole.

The years passed, and the King and his wife found GREAT happiness, and they forgot all about the magician's words. Their happiness increased when they were given a beautiful baby son. He was perfect in every way, and was called Hyacinth. But as he grew up, his nose grew faster than the rest of his body, and the King and his wife were saddened at the ridiculous length of their son's nose.

So that he would feel normal, his parents pulled their own noses, every day, to make them look longer.

All of the servants were sacked, and new servants, with the longest noses in the land, were taken on.

Prince Hyacinth's teacher taught him that all the greatest people in history had huge noses, as had all of the people that had ever invented anything worth having.

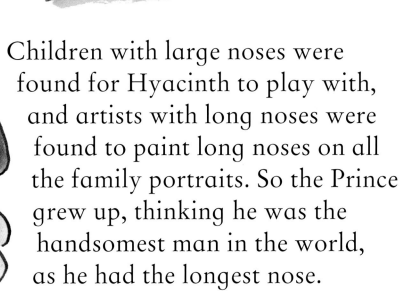

Children with large noses were found for Hyacinth to play with, and artists with long noses were found to paint long noses on all the family portraits. So the Prince grew up, thinking he was the handsomest man in the world, as he had the longest nose.

When he came of age, Hyacinth fell in love with the dear little Princess of the next door kingdom.

She loved him for who he was and didn't mind at all about his large nose. True, her nose was rather small, but his parents assured him that small noses were acceptable in girls, even a sign of beauty.

As the two kingdoms prepared for a marriage, nobody noticed the mouse, watching from the shadows. At the very moment Hyacinth met his dear little Princess, and bowed to kiss her hand, the mouse turned into the wicked magician, and whisked her away.

For months, Prince Hyacinth wandered both kingdoms searching for his Princess, tears splashing off the end of his nose, until one day, deep in a forest, he found her at last, locked in a glass palace.

He tried to break down the walls, but they were too strong. He could see her, but he couldn't touch her. Of course, the Princess also wanted to touch her Prince, and she stretched her hand out of a tiny window for him to kiss. But his nose was too long to allow his lips to reach. Hyacinth tried this way and that, but his nose always got in the way.

Sadly, he sat on a tussock of grass, and for the first time in his life, admitted to himself that his nose was too long.

That admission of the truth was enough to shatter the glass palace, for the truth is stronger than magic. The dear little Princess threw herself into his arms, but he pushed her away.

"You can't love me," he said. "Not with a nose like mine!" He tried to hide his nose in his hands, but to his amazement, it had shrunk to a third of its old size. You see, all sorts of good and magic things happen when you are honest with yourself.

The dear little Princess threw herself into his arms again.
"You have the most beautiful nose in the entire world!"
she said . . . and of course, they lived happily ever after.

FAIRY GIFTS

OVER a hill, in the land that no one could see, there lived a fairy queen and her four daughters. The Queen loved her daughters dearly, but, as is sometimes the case, she loved the youngest the most.

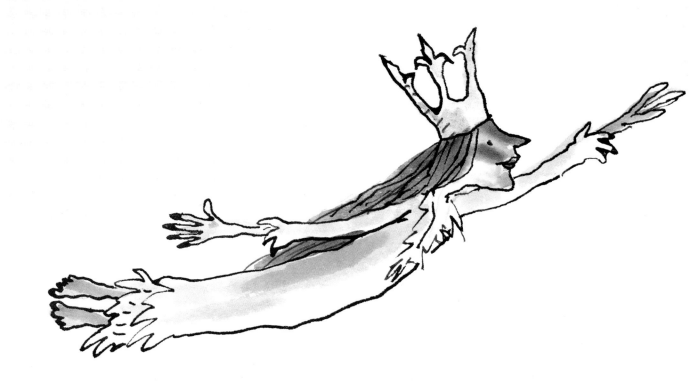

The Queen had everything that a queen should have: a castle, fine gardens, beauty, wit and a way with words. Of course, because she was a FAIRY queen, all of these things were magic.

As the girls grew up, they said they wanted to leave home and see the world for themselves.

"Very well," said the Queen, "but life away from home, on the other side of the hill, can be tricky. So to help you, I will give you each one of my gifts."

So she gave the eldest girl, Iris, the gift of beauty. To the next girl, Rose, she gave the gift of wit, and to the third girl, Poppy, she gave the gift of fine words.

Of course, the three girls were happy with their mother's gifts, and away they danced, to enjoy the world on the other side of the hill.

"But, Mama," said the youngest, whose name was Daisy, "what are you going to give to *me*?"

"My darling Daisy," the Queen replied, "I have nothing left! I have given away my beauty, my wit and my gift of fine words, so I really need you now to look after me."

Of course, Daisy was happy to do that for her mother, who had given so much to make her sisters happy. So the years rushed by, and the Queen and Daisy lived happily together in the castle and its fine garden.

But when they talked, they often wondered how Iris, Rose and Poppy were enjoying the world on the other side of the hill. One day, the Queen could stand it no longer.

"Darling Daisy," said the fairy Queen, "you must travel to the other side of the hill, seek out your sisters and bring news of them back to me. I long to know of their adventures, and how my gifts have aided them. I fear, though, I have no gifts left for you, and although I love you dearly, you must go as you are. Go now, hurry, and hurry back!"

Daisy thought she could see a tear in her mother's eye,
     so she lost no time putting on her best hat
           and setting off out into the world
               where everybody else lived,
                 on the other side of the hill.

Daisy climbed the hill all night, and in the morning, she was looking down at the city where everybody else lived. Soon she was in the crowded streets, calling her sisters' names.

"AH!" croaked an old woman with a blue face. "I heard say those three are living at the palace. They are all set to marry the three Princes, who are taken with their beauty, their wit and fine words. Go and look there!" The old woman pointed to a grand castle in the distance.

But when Daisy reached the palace, the guards would not let her in. "I'm looking for my sisters," she said. "I was told they live here. One is beautiful, one has wit and the other has fine words." "Oh, those three!" laughed the guards. "Those three aren't here now. Those three left months ago. You'll find them living together in Lumpen Lane."

Lumpen lane was in the poorest part of town, and Daisy found her sisters living in the poorest house imaginable. She was shocked at what she saw.

Iris was lying on a couch, with a box of cheap chocolates.

"Oh, Daisy," she wailed, "it is so good to see you. Because I was beautiful, I thought that nothing else was needed. I thought beauty was everything. So I did nothing, and got fat, then fatter. Soon I was ill, and my beauty just vanished. OOOOHHHH!"

"Poor Iris," said Daisy, turning to Rose.

"Oh, Daisy," wailed Rose, "my wit was the end of me. I turned everything into a joke. When my Prince asked me to marry him, I said that his happiness was sure, but mine was yet to be found. Of course it was a joke, but he married someone else and soon everybody tired of my wit."

"Poor, poor Rose," said Daisy, "and what of you, Poppy?"

"OOOOHHHH!" wailed Poppy. "All I used around the palace were fine words. I told the King how handsome he was, and everybody knew he looked like a pig. And I told the Queen what a fine lady she was, but everybody knew she had married a pig. Soon, nobody believed a word I said, and out I had to go."

Daisy thought for a while, and then hugged her
three sisters.
"You must come back over the hill with me,
and I will look after you all."
"But WHY?" cried the three girls. "We are
horrible!"
"No, you are not," said Daisy. "You
are my beautiful sisters, and I love
you. Come on!"
So Daisy led her sisters home, back
over the hill, to the
land that no one
could see, where
they lived happily
ever after with
their mother.

Sometimes, her mother apologised to Daisy for giving gifts to her sisters and not to her.

"But you gave Daisy the best gift of all," they cried. "You gave her the gift of love. Then you gave her another gift, the gift of letting her be herself!"

So, everybody loved Daisy, and princes came from far and wide to ask for her hand in marriage. But Daisy said "NO!", of course.

BEAUTY AND THE BEAST

ELSEWHERE and long ago, a merchant lived with his three daughters. The eldest was called Greedy, because she wanted everything, the middle one was called Envy, because she wanted everything that Greedy had, and the youngest was called Beauty, because she was one.

Well, times were hard, and the merchant lost all of his money, so he and his daughters had to leave their fine mansion and go to the very edge of the city to live in a tiny shed. Greedy and Envy complained bitterly, but Beauty tidied the shed and made it as comfortable as she could, to make everyone happy.

But Greedy and Envy complained all the more, so finally the merchant decided to go and find another fortune, in another country. Before he left, he promised to bring gifts for his daughters.

"OOOOH!" said Greedy. "I would like a golden box, full of the finest jewels, and a silk dress to wear them with!"

"OOOOH!" said Envy. "I want a box like that too, maybe with two silk dresses!"

"I'll have TEN dresses then," cried Greedy.

"Me too!" squealed Envy.

"And what would you like, darling?" the merchant asked Beauty, who was polishing the windows.

"As we have no garden here," said Beauty, "I would like a scented rose."

So the merchant went off, and he soon made another fortune.

As he was returning to his daughters, his ship was wrecked in a terrible storm. The merchant dragged himself on to dry land, having lost everything but his life. Of course, it was quite impossible now for him to buy presents for his daughters. Saddened at his loss, but happy to be alive, he stumbled into a forest.

As night fell, he came to a fine palace set in a beautiful garden. He rang the doorbell, hoping to beg a bed for the night. The door was opened by the ugliest thing that the merchant had ever seen. He had the face and body of an awful beast, but the fine clothes of a king. The merchant sprang back in fear, but the Beast smiled and held out a paw. When he smiled, the Beast did not look so frightening, so the merchant explained what had happened. The Beast stepped back, bowed and invited the merchant to enter.

Inside, invisible servants put more logs on the fire, and brought food. The merchant and the Beast ate, and swapped stories in the firelight. At bedtime, an invisible servant took the merchant's hand and led him to a warm and comfy bed, where he fell into a happy sleep.

When the merchant came down to breakfast, the Beast was already there, and in daylight, looking more terrible than ever. The merchant suddenly felt frightened and asked to be on his way. The Beast bowed, and said goodbye. As the merchant walked through the garden, he sniffed the scent of a rose. Looking around, he saw a beautiful bush covered with perfect roses. Remembering his youngest daughter's request, he plucked one as a present for her.

There was a TERRIBLE scream, and the merchant swung round to see the angry Beast rushing from the palace.
"I took you in, when you were cold!" he roared. "I gave you food, when you were hungry. I gave you a bed, when you were tired, and you repay my hospitality by stealing from me!
Why, I ought to gobble you up!"

The merchant fell to his knees, pleading for his life. "I am sorry, sorry, sorry!" he said. "I will do ANYTHING, but please don't gobble me up. I only wanted the rose as a gift for my youngest daughter, who is the sweetest person . . ."

The Beast quietened down, and looked thoughtful. "Very well," he said. "I won't gobble you up, IF you send your youngest daughter here to live with me." A beastly sadness came into his eyes. "Sometimes, you know, I do get awfully lonely."

"Yes, yes!" said the merchant, hurrying on his way, glad not to have been gobbled up. "Anything, anything, I promise!"

When the merchant arrived home, Greedy and Envy were angry to have no presents and they went away to sulk, but Beauty was delighted with her rose. It was JUST what she wanted. It was so perfect, she wanted to know all about it. At first, the merchant did not want to talk about the Beast, and the promise made to him, but at last Beauty got the full story out of him.

"Of course," said the merchant, "you don't HAVE to go and live with that Beast . . ."

"But I must," said Beauty, sadly. "For if a promise is made, it must be kept." Beauty packed a bag, and set off to live with the Beast.

The Beast was delighted with Beauty. She was kind, and helped around the palace, and even the invisible servants were happy because she was there. As the weeks passed, the Beast fell more and more in love with Beauty, and could not do enough to make her happy. He dressed her in fine clothes and jewels, and if she wanted the slightest thing he quickly did it. Well, weeks turned to months, and every day the Beast asked Beauty to marry him, and every day, Beauty said no. It was not only that she found him so ugly, it was that she had always dreamed of marrying a handsome prince. As more time passed, Beauty felt homesick and began to miss her father. She even began to miss Greedy and Envy. One day, she went to the Beast and asked if she could visit her old home for a few days.

"Of course you may, if that is what will make you happy," said the Beast, "but only on the condition that you will return to me after a week has passed." Beauty agreed, and the Beast knew that he could trust her. As a parting gift, he gave her an enchanted mirror. If she looked into it, she could see what was happening at the palace. He also gave her an enchanted ring, and told her if she were to turn it twice on her finger, she would be back at the palace in an instant.

When Beauty arrived home at the shed, her father was overjoyed to see her looking so well, and her sisters were amazed at her fine clothes and jewels.

"I would like clothes like that," said Greedy.

"Me too!" said Envy. They decided to persuade Beauty to stay much longer than the agreed week in order to give themselves enough time to trick her out of her clothes and jewels.

After two weeks had gone by, Beauty felt guilty about not returning to the Beast, so she looked into her mirror to see what was happening at the palace. To her horror, she saw the Beast lying in bed, with the invisible servants unable to help him. As Beauty had not returned, he was dying of a broken heart. Choking back her tears, Beauty turned the ring twice on her finger and flew back to him.

By the time she arrived at his bed, the Beast had died of sadness,
and Beauty knew in her heart that she had really loved him.

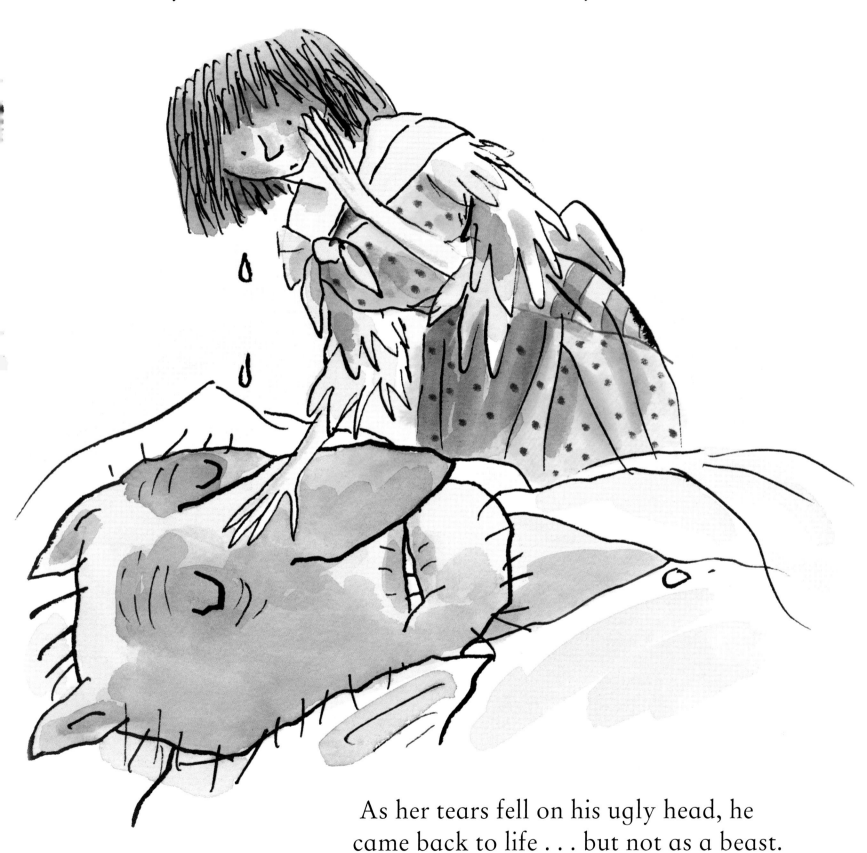

As her tears fell on his ugly head, he
came back to life . . . but not as a beast.

Slowly, he changed into a young prince, and a very handsome young prince at that, and the couple clung happily together.

The young Prince then explained to Beauty how long ago, a jealous fairy, angry that the handsome Prince would not marry her, had turned him into a hideous beast. He had to stay that way until somebody loved him in spite of his ugliness.

Beauty married her Prince, and they lived happily together for ever in the palace in the forest. Of course, the Prince bought a fine mansion for the merchant, and golden boxes of silk and jewels for Greedy and Envy. So everyone was happy until the end of days.